CW00386140

Electronic Keyboard Grade 8

Pieces & Technical Work
for Trinity College London exams

from 2013

Published by
Trinity College London
Registered office:
89 Albert Embankment
London SE1 7TP UK

T +44 (0)20 7820 6100
F +44 (0)20 7820 6161
E music@trinitycollege.co.uk
www.trinitycollege.co.uk

Registered in the UK
Company no. 02683033
Charity no. 1014792

Copyright © 2013 Trinity College London

First impression, February 2013

Unauthorised photocopying is illegal.
No part of this publication may be copied or reproduced in any
form or by any means without the prior permission of the publisher.

Printed in England by Halstan, Amersham, Bucks.

Czardas

Vittorio Monti
arr. Victoria Proudler

Voices: Fantasia, Piano, Piccolo, Strings, Violin
Style: Polka Pop
Split points: Left Voice bars 5–21 A♭³, 54–85 C⁴
             Accomp. bars 22–53 and 86–end B²
Other info: Fingered on bass chord setting to be used in bars 22–53 and 86–end.
             All voices to sound at written pitch using octave transpose as necessary
             (unless otherwise stated). Transposition is as follows:
             Bars 1–4 Octave -1 and to be played an octave higher
             Bars 5–21 Left Voice (LV) to be played and sound at written pitch, Right Voice (RV)
             Octave -1 to be played an octave higher
             Bars 54–69 RV and LV to both play and sound at written pitch
             Bars 70–85 LV Octave +1 and to be played an octave lower, RV to play at written
             pitch (piccolo to sound an octave higher).

Copyright © 2013 Trinity College London

* Bar 42 LH – suggested chord fingering A⁷/C♯ 3211 (thumb on both G and A) and A 532.

molto rall.

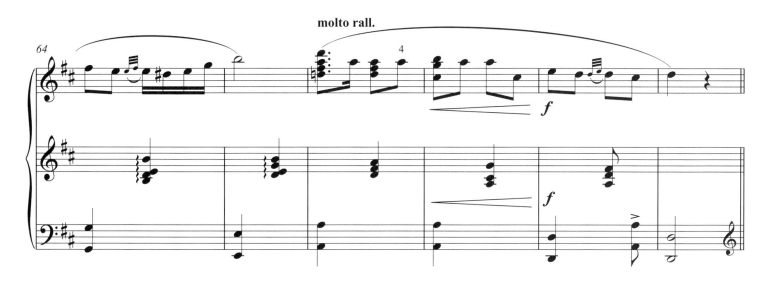

a tempo
To Fantasia & Piccolo (Picc. sounding an octave higher)

(LV Piano)
Use Left Hold if possible

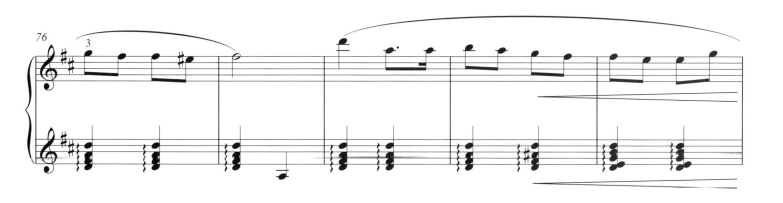

molto rall.

Sync.
start

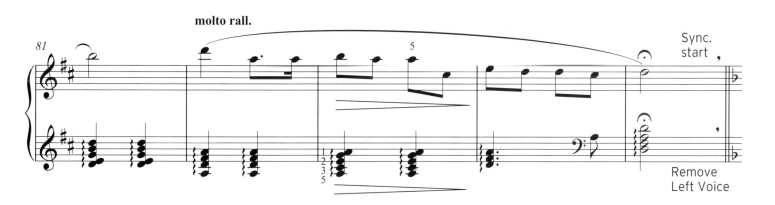

Remove
Left Voice

PLEASE SET UP FOR THE NEXT PIECE

Flight of the Bumblebee

Nikolai Rimsky-Korsakov

arr. Joanna Clarke

Voices: Fantasia, Fire Wire, Lead (Wire and Pop), Pad, Piano, Strings

Style: Dance or Trance or Techno

Split points: Accomp. bars 1-44 and 59-89 A^2, 45-57 $F\#^2$

Left Voice bars 7-21 and 39-44 A^2, 23-38 $F\#^3$, 45-55 E^3

Other info: Fingered on bass chord setting to be used throughout.

In bars 7-21 and 39-44 the Left Voice should be on and sound the accomp. chords played. If possible, the use of Left Hold is recommended for these bars. The written intro and ending should coincide with the use of the accomp. intro and ending.

Pitch bend range = 12 (hold top note and glide down to pitch of lower note).

Copyright © 2013 Trinity College London

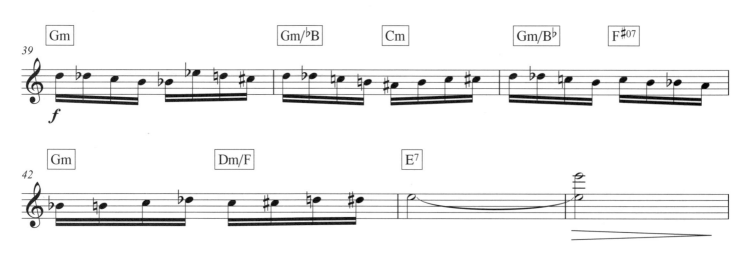

* The pause should be held until the end of the Accomp. Ending

PLEASE SET UP FOR THE NEXT PIECE

Feeling Good

Leslie Bricusse/Anthony Newley
arr. Victoria Proudler

Voices: _____

Style: _____

Other info: Fingered on bass chord setting to be used from bar 11.
Left Voice is suggested for the LH, changing split point
and octave as required.

[♩. = 65–70]

Accomp. and Rhythm off suggested

*Candidates should refer to the current syllabus
requirements for Own Interpretation pieces.

Copyright © 1964 Concord Music Ltd.
of Suite 2.07, Plaza 535 Kings Road, London SW10 0SZ
International Copyright Secured
All Rights Reserved. Used by Permission.

Left Voice suggested,
with Accomp. on

PLEASE SET UP FOR THE NEXT PIECE

Palladio

Karl Jenkins
arr. Joanna Clarke

Voices:	Harp, Orchestral, Strings
Style:	Dance
Split point:	Left Voice bars 27–33 E♭³
Pedal:	Pedal function should be set to Fill
Other info:	Full fingered (or AI full keyboard) chord accompaniment setting to be used where Accomp. on is instructed.

© Copyright 1996 by Boosey & Hawkes Music Publishers Ltd.
This arrangement © Copyright 2012 by Boosey & Hawkes Music Publishers Ltd. Arranged by permission.

Kissing a Fool

Words and Music by George Michael
arr. Nancy Litten

Voices:	Brass section, Piano, Sax. section, Strings
Style:	Acoustic Jazz (bars 1–39 and 51–end), 40s Big Band (bars 40–50)
Split points:	Accomp. G^2
	Left Voice G^2
Pedal:	Pedal function should be set to Fill
Other info:	Left Hold should be on throughout if possible.
	Left Voice chords should be played an octave lower. All voices to sound at written pitch using octave transpose as necessary.
	Quavers marked as duplets should be played straight not swung.

Copyright © 1985 Big Geoff Overseas Ltd (PRS) administered by Warner/Chappell Music International Ltd
This arrangement © 2013 Big Geoff Overseas Ltd (PRS) administered by Warner/Chappell Music International Ltd
Warner/Chappell Music Ltd, London W6 8BS
Reproduced by permission of Faber Music Ltd and Alfred Music Publishing Co., Inc. All Rights Reserved.

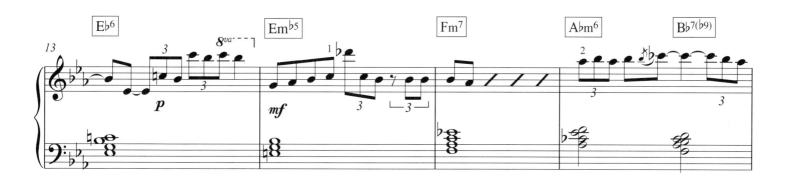

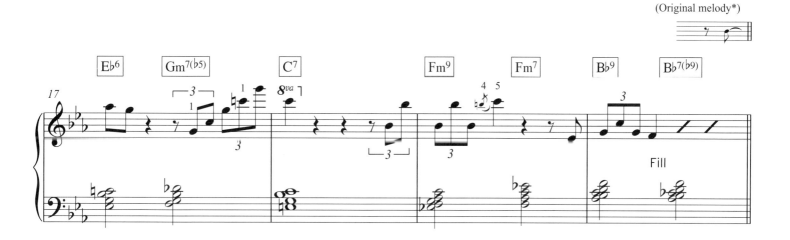

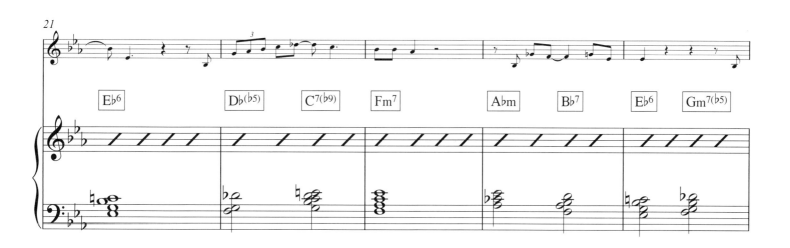

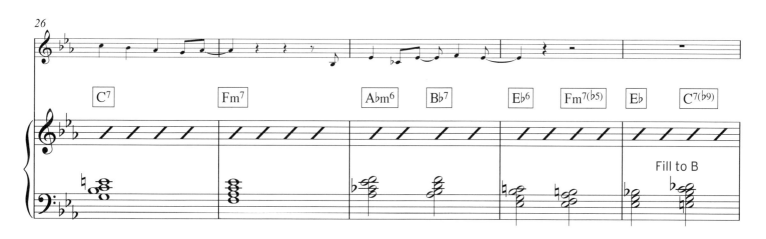

* The original melody line is shown as a guide for improvisation.

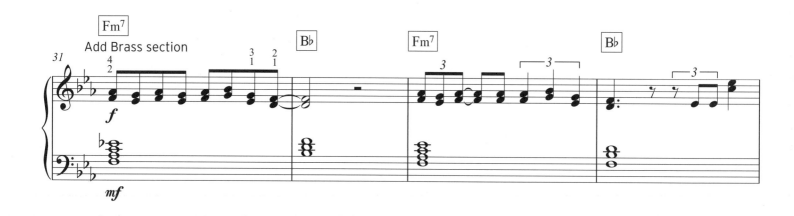

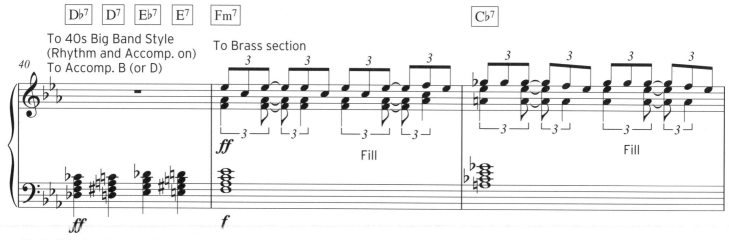

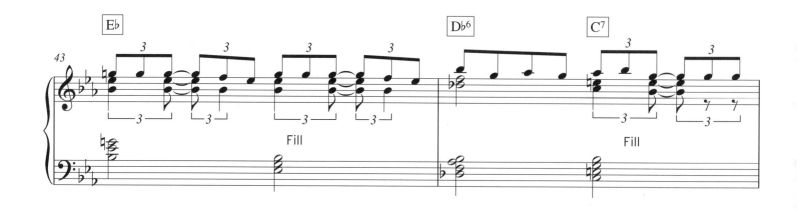

PLEASE SET UP FOR THE NEXT PIECE

Spring Dance

Martin Thiselton

Voices: Flute, Harp, Strings, Trumpet, Violin
Style: $\frac{6}{8}$ Folk Rock (bars 1–23 and 52–91), Jazz Waltz or $\frac{9}{8}$ Folk Rock (bars 24–51)
Split points: Accomp. bars 1–16 and 24–end Ab[2], 17–23 D[3]
Left Voice bars 5–8 and 13–16 Ab[2], 17–23 D[3], 52–69 Ab[2]
Other info: Fingered on bass chord setting to be used.
Left Hold should be used if possible in bars 5–8, 13–23 and 52–69.
Left Voice chords should be played an octave lower. All voices to sound at written pitch using octave transpose as necessary.

Copyright © 2013 Trinity College London

Technical Work

Candidate should prepare EITHER section i) Scales and Chord Knowledge OR section ii) Exercises. Section i) must be performed from memory; the music may be used for Section ii).

Please see the current syllabus for any further information as requirements can change.

i) Scales and Chord Knowledge

The following scales to be performed in piano voice with auto-accompaniment off, hands together (unless otherwise stated), ♩ = 140, *legato* and *mf*:

Db, E, G and Bb major (two octaves)

C#, E, G and Bb minor (two octaves): harmonic *and* melodic

Chromatic scales in similar motion starting on *any* note (two octaves)

Chromatic scale with hands a minor third apart starting on Bb and Db (two octaves)

Major pentatonic scale starting on E and Db, straight and swing rhythm, hands separately (two octaves)

Blues scale starting on C# and G#, straight and swing rhythm, right hand only (two octaves)

Db major scale (two octaves)

E major scale (two octaves)

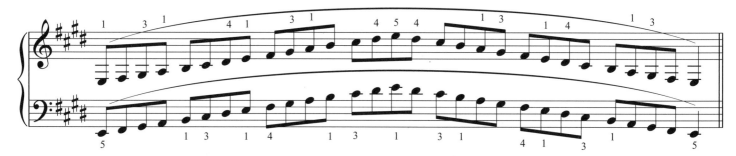

G major scale (two octaves)

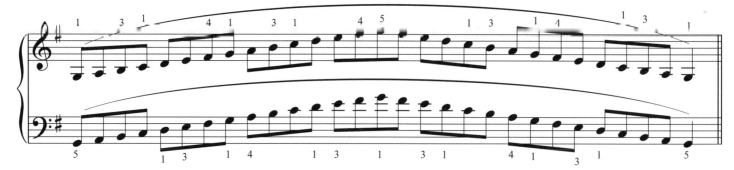

Bb major scale (two octaves)

C# minor scale: harmonic (two octaves)

C# minor scale: melodic (two octaves)

E minor scale: harmonic (two octaves)

E minor scale: melodic (two octaves)

G minor scale: harmonic (two octaves)

G minor scale: melodic (two octaves)

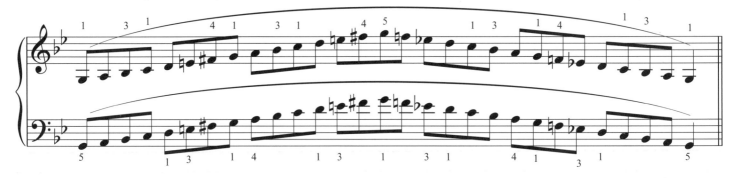

B♭ minor scale: harmonic (two octaves)

B♭ minor scale: melodic (two octaves)

Chromatic scale in similar motion starting on any note e.g. D♭ or E (two octaves)

Chromatic scale with hands a minor third apart starting on B♭ and D♭ (two octaves)

Major pentatonic scale starting on E (two octaves), straight and swing rhythm

Right hand

Left hand

Major pentatonic scale starting on D♭ (two octaves), straight and swing rhythm

Right hand

Left hand

Blues scale starting on C♯ (two octaves), straight and swing rhythm

Right hand

Blues scale starting on G♯ (two octaves), straight and swing rhythm

Right hand

The following to be performed using piano voice with auto-accompaniment off:

Triad of D♭, E, G and B♭ major, C♯, E, G and B♭ minor in all inversions (to be played in the left hand)
Chords of C♯^{o7}, E^{o7}, G^{o7}, B♭^{o7}, D♭^{add9}, E^{add9}, G^{add9}, B♭^{add9}, C♯m$^{7(♭5)}$, Em$^{7(♭5)}$, Gm$^{7(♭5)}$, B♭m$^{7(♭5)}$ in root position only (to be played with the bass note in the left hand and the chord in the right hand)
Perfect, imperfect and plagal cadence in B♭ major and G minor

D♭ major

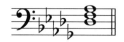  

E major

  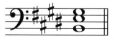

G major

B♭ major

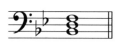 

C♯ minor

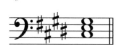  

E minor

  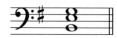

G minor

Bb minor

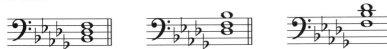

C#°7

E°7

G°7

Bb°7

Db add9

E add9

G add9

Bb add9

C#m7(b5)

Em7(b5)

Gm7(b5)

Bb7(b5)

Perfect cadence in Bb major

Plagal cadence in Bb major

Imperfect cadence in Bb major

Perfect cadence in G minor

Plagal cadence in G minor

Imperfect cadence in G minor

ii) Exercises

Candidate to prepare **all** three exercises; only two exercises will be heard in the exam.

1. Smoothly Does It – for right hand legato octaves and left hand fingered on bass chords

Voice: Strings
Style: $\frac{6}{8}$ Ballad
Split point: Accomp. G^2
Other info: Fingered on bass chord setting to be used

2. All Fired Up – for broken chord playing and stride bass

Voice: Piano
Style: None

3. Ornamental Cascade – for dexterity with ornaments and use of the thumb

Voices: Flute, Violin
Style: Rumba
Split point: Accomp. G^2
Other info: Fingered on bass chord setting to be used